Sammy's Mommy Has Cancer

by Sherry Kohlenberg
illustrated by Lauri Crow

Magination Press • New York

This book is dedicated to my son Sammy
and my husband Larry, with love, forever.

Library of Congress Cataloging-in-Publication Data
Kohlenberg, Sherry.
    Sammy's mommy has cancer / by Sherry Kohlenberg ; illustrated by
Lauri Crow
        p.   cm.
    Summary: Sammy's mommy receives treatment for cancer, goes into
the hospital for surgery, recovers at home, and shares her
continuing love for him.
    ISBN 0-945354-56-8 (cloth). — ISBN 0-945354-55-X (paper)
    [1. Cancer—Fiction.]   I. Crow, Lauri, ill. II. Title.
PZ7.K82334Sam 1993
[E]—dc20   93-22773
                                                                 CIP
                                                                  AC

Manufactured in the United States of America

10 9 8 7 6 5 4 3 2 1

Introduction

When I was diagnosed with breast cancer at 34 years old, my son, Sammy, was 18 months old. My husband and I searched for a book to help us explain to Sammy why and how this horrible disease disrupted our lives. We wanted a book to share as a family to help guide Sammy and us through surgery, chemotherapy, and recovery. Though there were books explaining the death of a parent to a child, we couldn't find a book that dealt with the sorrow, hopes, and even small joys that our family was experiencing in our struggle against breast cancer. This book was born out of frustration and a desire to keep Sammy a close part of everything that was happening to our family.

I hope that this book accomplishes three things. First, I wanted Sammy to know that cancer was something that could happen to any family, that it wasn't something that anyone caused, and that we were still a normal family even though I was sick. Second, I wanted to guide Sammy through the various treatments that I was going through so that he would know what to expect and suggest to him ways that he could help. Lastly, even though we knew that this was a horrible disease and we didn't know what the outcome would be, there were still times for happiness and even celebrations—when tumors shrank, when I healed from surgery and my strength returned, when our lives returned to what they were like before I was diagnosed with breast cancer. These very important, special moments of shared happiness are represented at the end of the book when Sammy takes off my scarf and feels my hair growing back.

Throughout the last three years, we used a handmade copy of this book with Sammy. At times Sammy wanted us to read it to him every night. He recognized when things happened in our lives that were just like what happens in the book. As he got older and his ability to understand grew, the book became something he could rely on.

My love for Sammy inspired me to write this book. I hope that this love for my son is reflected in these pages and is helpful to other parents and their children.

Activities

Open communication with our son has been the most important activity throughout my family's struggle with cancer. We always took our cues from Sammy. We answered all his questions but didn't give him more information than he asked for. In time, Sammy asked every question that adults asked, and we answered them as straightforwardly and honestly as we could.

The activities listed below are other ways we included our son. They are divided into sections of before, during, and after treatments. You may not feel that some activities are appropriate for your son or daughter. Some you may use as a starting point for other ways of interacting with your child. You know your own children. Listen to them and they'll let you know how far to go.

Before Treatment

— Visit the doctor, clinic and/or hospital with your child before your treatment. Let them talk to the doctors and ask them questions and see that the place where Mommy is getting treated is safe and nonthreatening. Show your child the equipment that will be used during treatment and a hospital room like the one Mommy will be in while recovering from surgery.

— Go with your child to his/her daycare or school and let them tell their teacher what is happening to Mommy. Call the school ahead of time to warn the teacher. This allows your child to feel comfortable with the situation, that it isn't something that he or she must hide or be ashamed of. Also, talk with parents of your child's friends and tell them to expect open communication from your child.

— Let your child draw what they think a cancer cell looks like and let them "zap" it with their favorite color crayon.

During Treatment

— Let your child pick a simple object that they can easily bring to Mommy to let Mommy know that they love her. Rocks from the playground, a pretty picture from a magazine, a simple drawing, or perhaps a flower from a local shop on the way to the hospital could be used.

— Let your child simply sit or lie next to Mommy and snuggle.

— When Mommy is feeling well enough, have a picnic in Mommy's hospital room.

After Treatment

— After surgery, your child may be curious about your "boo boo." When I had healed, I let Sammy see and touch my scar. He seemed comforted that it didn't hurt anymore and that it wasn't as bad as he had imagined it.

— Let your child do the physical therapy exercises with you.

— Do some simple gardening, reaffirming life.

Sammy lives with his mommy and daddy in a little white house with a big oak tree in front.

Sammy's mommy goes to work in an office.

His daddy works in his office at home.

Sammy goes to school where he has lots of friends.

Sammy likes to play with dinosaurs, his favorite toys.

One day Sammy's mommy goes to the doctor. The doctor tells her that she has a sickness called cancer.

Everyone's body is made of good cells. Sammy's mommy doesn't feel sick, but there are bad cancer cells growing in her body that aren't supposed to be there.
Cancer isn't anybody's fault.

When Mommy and Daddy come home from the doctor, they tell Sammy about Mommy's cancer. Mommy and Daddy are sad. Sammy is sad, too.

When Mommy is sad, Sammy hugs her and gives her a kiss. This is how Sammy says, "I love you."

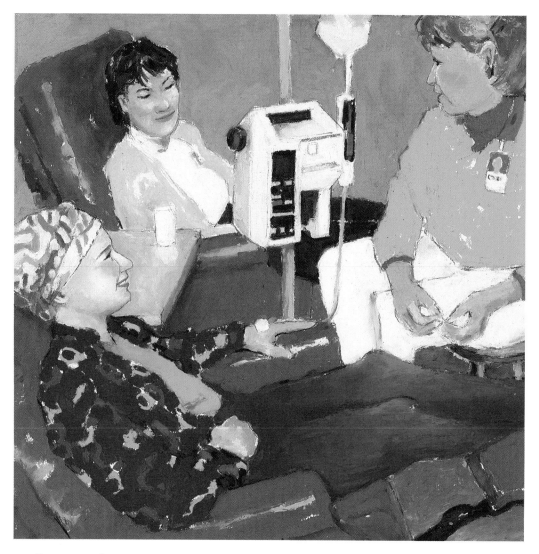

Sammy's mommy goes to the clinic. The doctor gives her medicine to make the cancer cells go away.

The medicine to fight cancer is very strong. It sometimes makes Mommy feel sick. She stays in bed. Daddy takes care of her and Sammy helps.

The medicine is so strong, it makes Sammy's mommy's hair fall out. Without her hair, she still looks like Mommy. But she looks different, too.

Mommy says she looks like Sammy when he was a teeny, tiny baby. Sammy looks at little babies. Some of them don't have any hair either.

Mommy wears pretty scarves on her head.

Sometimes she wears a wig that looks like her hair, but at night she takes it off.

One day Sammy and Daddy take Mommy to the hospital for surgery to take the cancer away.

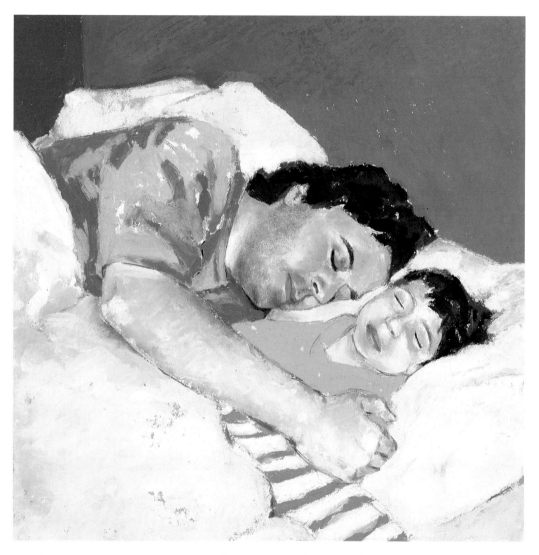

Sammy sometimes sleeps with his daddy when Mommy goes to the hospital.

When Sammy's mommy comes home from the hospital, she stays in bed. She needs to rest while her body works hard to make her well.

Sometimes Sammy sits in bed with Mommy. They read or watch television.

Sammy's mommy exercises to get stronger. Sammy exercises with her.

Pretty soon Mommy is moving around like she did before she stayed in the hospital.

When Sammy's mommy goes back to her doctors, they tell her the cancer is gone. She will go back for checkups in case the cancer comes back.

Everyone is very happy.

One day, Sammy's mommy takes off her scarf.

Sammy touches her head. And he can feel her hair growing.

Glossary

Cancer Like winding weeds through a beautiful garden that stop plants from growing wonderful vegetables or colorful flowers, cancer is a disease that appears in a person's body and stops the body from doing what it is supposed to do. Weeds that are not stopped can harm a garden. Cancer must also be treated to stop it from harming the person's body. Sadly, it is a lot harder to stop cancer than it is to stop weeds from growing.

Cells Every person's body is made of tiny cells that are so small you can't see them. Each cell is like a tiny grain of sand. A grain of sand doesn't look like much, but a bunch of tiny grains of sand make up a whole beach. It takes a bunch of tiny cells to make up a person's whole body.

Checkups Every person's body works in much the same way. People go to doctors for a checkup to make sure that their bodies are working the way they should. Most of the time the doctors find that a person's body is working just fine. When the doctor finds something that isn't working right, the doctor tells the person what they should do to help get their body right.

Clinics Clinics are places where doctors and nurses work on particular problems. At an ear clinic, doctors treat ear problems. At a bone clinic, they work on bones. At a cancer clinic, they work on cancer.

Doctors Doctors are people who study the human body for a very long time and know how it is supposed to work. They help people who are well stay healthy, and they help people who are sick get better.

Hospitals Hospitals are usually large buildings with lots of doctors, nurses, patients, and other people. Hospitals have many clinics, rooms for people who have to stay in the hospital overnight, waiting rooms where people can sit and read while waiting for the doctor, restaurants, and lots of other things. Hospitals can be very busy with people running around doing many things.

Medicine Medicine is what a doctor gives a person to help them get better. Some medicines are a pill, some a liquid. Some are given with a shot, some through a pump that a person is hooked up to for a few hours. Chemotherapy is medicine given by a doctor to help a person fight cancer.

Radiation Radiation is a treatment that some people get to fight cancer. When a person gets radiation, they go into a room with a big machine. The machine is aimed at the part of the person's body that has cancer. Radiation, which you can't see, comes out of the machine and goes into the person's body to attack the cancer without hurting the person.

Sickness When a person's body isn't doing what it is supposed to be doing, that person may be sick. Some people with a sickness, like a flu or an ear infection, feel really bad. Other sicknesses, like some cancers, may not make the person feel bad right away but are really hurting the person's body.

Surgery Surgery is what doctors do when they remove cancer from a person's body. Surgery usually leaves a scar, like a bad cut, which may be sore at first but then gets better.

Resources

Books

Baker, L. *You and Leukemia.* Philadelphia, W. B. Saunders Company, 1988.

Bombeck, E. *I Want to Grow Hair, I Want to Grow Up, I Want to Go to Boise.* New York, Harper and Row. Finds the emotion and the humor in having cancer while suggesting coping skills.

Brack, P. *Moms Don't Get Sick.* Aberdeen, SD, Melius Publishing, 1990. A mother and child's relationship and its evolution through the challenge of breast cancer.

Chamberlain, S. *My ABC Book of Cancer.* San Francisco, Synergistic Press, 1990. Uses the alphabet to talk about hospital experiences.

Heegaard, M. *When Someone Very Special Dies.* Minneapolis, Woodland Press, 1991. A coloring/work book to help children express and cope with feelings of loss and grief.

Holden, D. *Gran-Gran's Best Trick.* New York, Magination Press, 1989. A child copes with her grandfather's illness and death from cancer.

LeShan, E. *Learning to Say Good-Bye: When a Parent Dies.* New York, Avon Books. How to deal with death, adults, and your own feelings about going on living.

LeShan, E. *When a Parent Is Very Sick.* Boston, Joy Street Books, 1986.

Little, J. *Mama's Going to Buy You a Mockingbird.* New York, Puffin Books, 1984. Two young children whose father is ill with cancer.

Mellonie, B. & Ingpen, R. *Lifetimes: A Beautiful Way to Explain Death to Children.* New York, Bantam Books, 1983. Uses the life cycles of plants and animals to show how humans have life cycles also.

Mills, J. C. *Gentle Willow.* New York, Magination Press, 1993. Helps children cope with their own life-threatening illness or with the death of someone they care about.

Parkinson, C. S. *My Mommy Has Cancer.* Rochester, NY, Park Press, 1991. A child's experiences when his mother is hospitalized for cancer.

Schulz, C. M. *Why, Charlie Brown, Why?* New York, Topper Books, 1990. A young girl with leukemia goes to the hospital, then returns to school full of hope.

Silverstein, A. & Silverstein, V. B. *Cancer: Can It Be Stopped?* New York, J. B. Lippincott, 1987.

Swenson, J. H. & Kunz, R. B. *Cancer: The Whispered Word.* Minneapolis, Dillon Press, 1986.

Videotapes

"Why, Charlie Brown, Why? A Story About What Happens When a Friend Is Very Ill." Animation helps young children understand their friend's leukemia and special needs.

"PEI: Tangles in a Threat." Animation stresses feeling of fear, separation and curiosity about death. Upbeat ending asserts, "It's okay if it's cancer, good things can still happen."

"What Do I Tell the Children?" Joanne Woodward discusses how to tell children about illness and loss.

Organizations

American Cancer Society, National Legislative Office, 316 Pennsylvania Avenue, SE, #200, Washington, DC 20003; 800-227-2345

California Breast Cancer Organization, 3381 Brownlea Circle, Sacramento, CA 95842; 619-586-7858

Cancer Care, Inc., 1180 Avenue of the Americas, 2d floor, New York, NY 10036; 212-221-3300

Centers for Disease Control—CCDPHP, 1600 Clifton Road, MS-K52, Atlanta, GA 30333; 404-639-3311

National Alliance of Breast Cancer Organizations (NABCO), 1180 Avenue of the Americas, New York, NY 10036; 212-719-0152

National Breast Cancer Coalition, P.O. Box 66373, Washington, DC 20035; 202-296-7477

National Cancer Institute, Office of Cancer Communication, Building 31, Room 10A24, Bethesda, MD 20892; 800-4-CANCER

National Coalition for Cancer Survivorship, 1010 Wayne Avenue, #300, Silver Spring, MD 20910; 505-764-9956

National Women's Health Network, 1325 G Street, NW, Washington, DC 20005

Virginia Breast Cancer Foundation, P.O. Box 17884, Richmond, VA 23226; 804-285-1200

Y-ME National Organization for Breast Cancer Information and Support, 18220 Harwood Avenue, Homewood, IL 60430; 708-799-8338 or 800-221-2141